MOBY SHINOBI

NINJA ON THE FARM

by Luke Flowers

SCHOLASTIC INC.

FOR GRANDPA BOB

Thanks for training me for life's adventures,
cheering me through wins and failures,
and teaching me to always serve others.
You are my hero. Forever.

Library of Congress Cataloging-in-Publication Data

Names: Flowers, Luke, author, illustrator. Title: Ninja on the farm / by Luke Flowers.
Description: New York, NY : Scholastic Inc., 2017. | Series: Scholastic reader. Level 1 | Series:
Moby Shinobi ; [1] | Summary: Moby Shinobi wants to put his ninja skills to use by helping a farmer in
need, but everything goes wrong until he finds just the right job. Identifiers: LCCN 2016028730|
ISBN 9780545935371 (paperback) | ISBN 9780545935388 (hardcover) Subjects: | CYAC:
Stories in rhyme. | Ninja—Fiction. | Helpfulness—Fiction. | Farm life—Fiction. | Humorous stories. |
BISAC: JUVENILE FICTION / Readers / Beginner. | JUVENILE FICTION / Action &
Adventure / General. | JUVENILE FICTION / Animals / Farm Animals. Classification: LCC
PZ8.3.F672 Nin 2017 | DDC [E]—dc23 LC record available at https://lccn.loc.gov/2016028730

10 9 8 7 6 5 4 3 2 1   17 18 19 20 21

Printed in Malaysia   108
First printing 2017
Book design by Steve Ponzo

Hi-yah! Hello! Come watch me train!
I love to use my ninja brain!

Swoop! Swipe! Snag! I am ninja quick!

Spin! Flip! Whoosh! Watch my super kick!

Run! Jump! Go! I have ninja speed!

Farm life starts with a rooster's crow.
Now to the chicken coop we go.

Moby thinks of how ninjas swoop!
He creeps into the chicken coop.

Moby thinks of ninja spin school!
He tries to choose the perfect tool.

Please give my pigs these pails of slop.
Then fill their water to the top!

Moby thinks of a ninja jump.
He stands tall on the water pump.

The farmer's dog lets out a YELP!
Moby wonders who could need help.

27

So Moby thinks of rope to throw.
Now it is time to go, go, go!